Disney

THE PROUD FAMILY

LOUDER and PROUDER

Based on the episode written by Calvin Brown Jr.
Adapted by Frank Berrios

For information address Disney Press, 1200 Grand Central Avenue, Glendale, California 91201.

Printed in the United States of America   First Paperback Edition, September 2022   10 9 8 7 6 5 4 3 2 1

FAC-029261-21351   Library of Congress Control Number: 2021945907   ISBN 978-1-368-08091-0

For more Disney Press fun, visit www.disneybooks.com

Disney PRESS
Los Angeles • New York

During a tight basketball game, the Proud Snackers rallied to defeat the Boulevardez Hardhats! As Oscar Proud, coach of the Proud Snackers, celebrated afterward with a slice of pizza, he was interrupted by Wizard Kelly. The Wizard was a retired professional basketball player as well as a successful businessman. Everything he touched turned to gold!

"Good game," said the Wizard. "Too bad you're not going to win the championship."

The Wizard proudly introduced his new team.

"Meet the Wizard Kelly All-Stars, made up of the children of all-time NBA greats," he bragged. "Not only is there my son, Lil Wizard, but there's Lil Jordan, Lil Shaq, Lil Dirk, and Lil LeBron!"

"I bet my team will beat your team!" said Oscar. "And if I win, I get to live like you for a week. The house, the cars, and the money. And you gotta live like me!"

"Okay, Proud, you've got a bet," replied the Wizard.

Suddenly, Michael, the Proud Snackers' star player, tripped.
"Oww, my knee! My knee!" he cried.

Oscar was sunk. What was he going to do now?

Back home, the twins, BeBe and CeCe, were making a mess!

"Where's Penny? She's supposed to be watching them," said Oscar.

When he and Trudy walked into the living room, they spotted Penny with a friend named Kareem.

Trudy reminded Penny of the rule: No boys in the house unsupervised.

Kareem responded by complimenting Trudy, but Oscar wasn't having it. "Quit trying to butter up my wife," said Oscar. "Stand up, son, so I can look you in the eye."

"Yessir," replied Kareem. When he stood up, Oscar couldn't believe how tall he was! Oscar's prayers were answered. "Follow me to the court, Kareem, ol' boy!"

"You don't have to do this," said Penny. "Don't let my daddy pressure you. Be true to yourself. If you don't want to play basketball, just tell him."

When Oscar saw how terrible Kareem was on the court, his dreams were dashed. "That kid is a complete waste of height," he said.

Suddenly, they heard someone else outside making shot after shot. To their surprise, it was Penny!

"Where did you learn to shoot like that?" asked Oscar.

"You taught me. When I was a little girl," replied Penny.

"With that jumper, you're the new shooting guard for the Proud Snackers!" exclaimed Oscar.

"But I don't like basketball," she said.

"Please, Penny, please!" begged Oscar. "I can't lose to the Wizard! You gotta help me. There's no way that the Snackers can win the championship without you!"

"Okay, Daddy. I'll do it. But I'm only doing it for you. Not me."

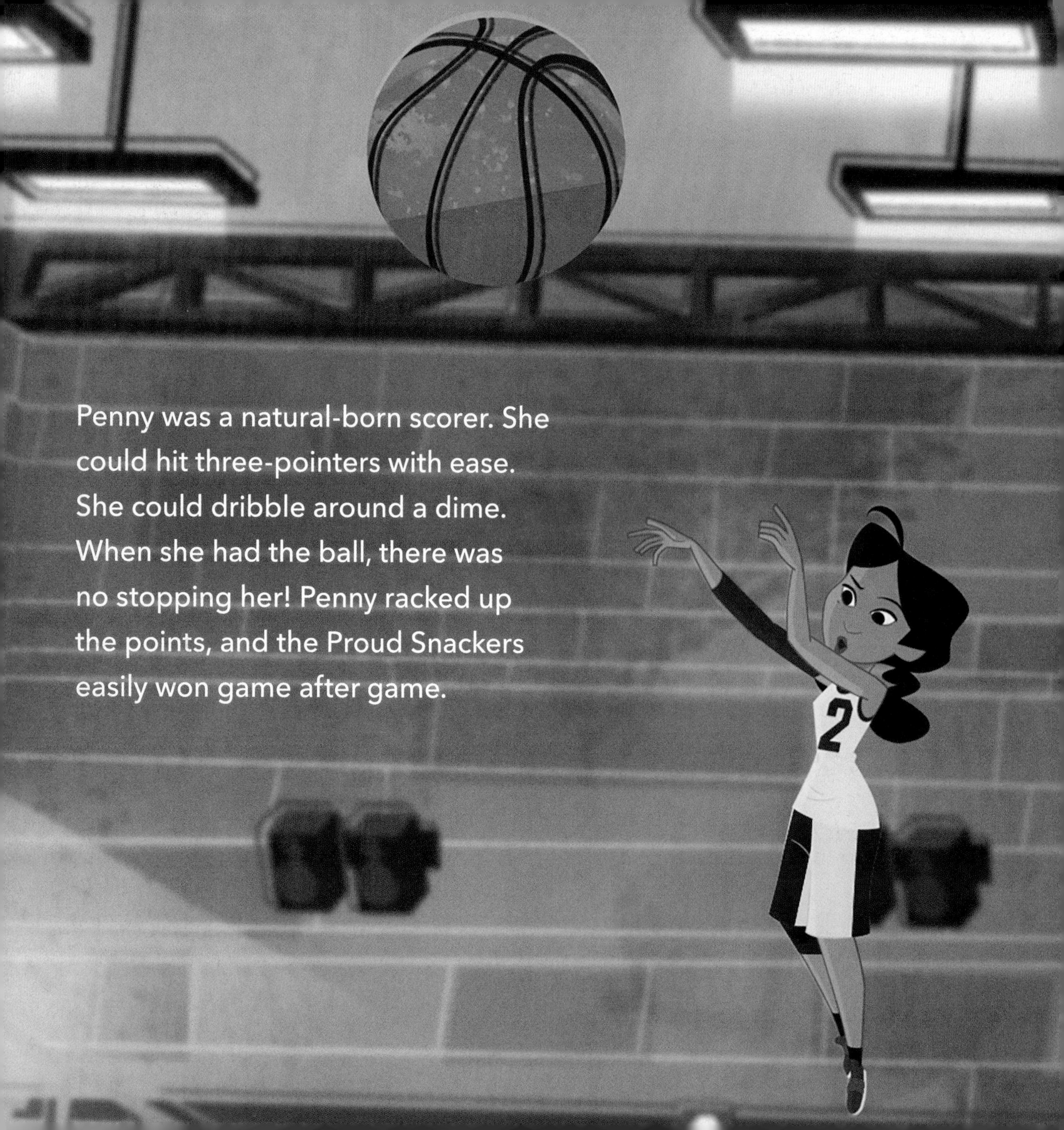

Penny was a natural-born scorer. She could hit three-pointers with ease. She could dribble around a dime. When she had the ball, there was no stopping her! Penny racked up the points, and the Proud Snackers easily won game after game.

HALOS
08
PROUD
SNACKERS
68
2

Meanwhile, Kareem waited and waited to spend time with Penny. He waited at the library, but she never showed. When he tried to catch her at home, she was at basketball practice. "Tell Penny I stopped by," he said to her mom.

With Penny on the squad, the Proud Snackers continued to win big.

She was the star player, but she didn't want to be there.

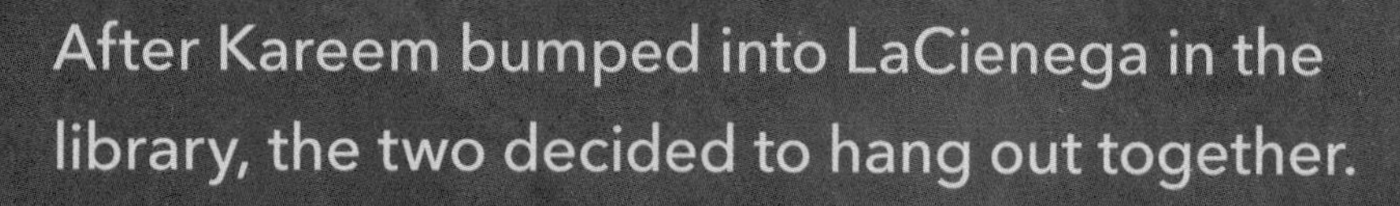

After Kareem bumped into LaCienega in the library, the two decided to hang out together.

Penny's friend Dijonay confronted LaCienega at lunch.

"LaCienega, you know that Penny and Kareem are boo'd up, and you over there trying to be messy!" she said.

"I don't know what you're talking about," LaCienega replied with pseudo innocence. "Kareem and I are just in a book club . . . of two."

Zoey interrupted the discussion. "We're going to Penny's game tonight. Are you guys coming?"

"I'd love to be there, but I don't think I can make it," said LaCienega as she got up to leave. "Kareem invited me to his concert."

Penny was upset about what LaCienega had said. She didn't notice Kareem watching from the sideline as she practiced her jump shot.

"What happened to you at the library the other day?" he asked.

"Oh snap, I forgot. My bad. Things have been crazy," answered Penny. "Practice every day. Games every evening. I'm sorry."

"I thought you didn't like basketball," said Kareem. "You don't have to do this. Don't let your daddy pressure you. Be true to yourself. If you don't want to play basketball, tell him you don't want to play."

"You're throwing my words back in my face," said Penny. "But that's easy for you, 'cause you can't ball like this."

As she took a shot, Kareem snagged the ball. Then he easily performed a 360-degree slam dunk. Penny was shocked. Kareem actually had serious basketball skills! He had only pretended to be bad so he wouldn't have to play on the team.

At the game later that day, Penny was being outplayed by the Wizard Kelly All-Stars. They were really good!

Oscar didn't care. He only cared about winning. "Penny, wake up! Play some defense!" he yelled.

"Daddy, I don't care about beating the Wizard!" she confessed. "That's your dream. I never wanted to do this!"

Oscar had a tantrum.
"If you don't want to play
Proud Snacker basketball,
then pack up your stuff and
go home!" he screamed.
"Just leave!"

"Fine! C'mon, y'all! Let's
go get pizza!" replied Penny.
The rest of the team quickly
grabbed their stuff and
followed Penny off the court.

After his concert, Kareem spotted Penny in the audience.

"What are you doing here?" he asked.

"I'm not doing the basketball thing anymore," replied Penny.

"So you took your own advice," he noted.

"Yep. Look, we're going to get some pizza. Wanna come?" asked Penny.

Kareem smiled. "Let's get out of here," he said.

Unfortunately, Oscar lost the basketball bet. He was forced to work at the Wizard's movie theater.

"I need eight tickets, Daddy. Can we get in free?" asked Penny.

"Not with that boy on your arm," replied Oscar as they raced into the theater.